This Book Belongs To:

....

....

Stories
to Share

Stories
to Share

Bath • New York • Singapore • Hong Kong • Cologne • Delhi
Melbourne • Amsterdam • Johannesburg • Auckland • Shenzhen

Illustrated by Alison Atkins

This edition published by Parragon in 2014

Parragon
Chartist House
15-17 Trim Street
Bath BA1 1HA, UK
www.parragon.com

ISBN 978-1-4454-1978-7

Printed in China

Contents

Poor Humphrey   10
Jan Payne

Ella's Playhouse   14
Clive Batkin

The Selfish Puppy   18
Gaby Goldsack

Smile, Please!   22
Jillian Harker

The Very Serious Lion Cub   26
Gaby Goldsack

Poor Humphrey

Humphrey was a baby rhino and he wasn't at all happy. He had a nobbly thing on his face instead of a spike, and he didn't like it one little bit.

So Humphrey refused to go out unless he was wearing his cardboard box to cover it.

"How can I wash behind your ears, you silly thing?" Mum would laugh when she tried to give him a bath. And if he got a cold and tried to blow his nose, well – you've never seen such a mess!

One day,
Humphrey was
fed up staying
indoors. He just
had to go outside.

He stumbled along
trying to look at things
through the holes in his
box. He saw a lizard on a
rock. He sniffed a red flower
on a bush. He watched an army
of ants carrying things on their backs.

Suddenly, Humphrey heard giggling. He felt a tug
at his box.

"Oi!" he shouted. "Give that back Monkey."

Humphrey was cross. He put the box back on his
head. Then he heard singing and laughing. It instantly
cheered him up.

Into the clearing came a group of baby rhinos. And guess what! They were all wearing cardboard boxes on their heads, just like Humphrey. They stopped when they saw him and asked him to play with them.

Humphrey stayed in the clearing all afternoon, playing games, singing songs and telling rhino jokes.

One day not long after, Humphrey put on his best box to go out. When he did this, it ripped right down the front. He felt the front of his face. There was something there. Something sharp.

He went to the water's edge and looked at his reflection. Woah! There it was, plain as the nose on your face. The "nobbly thing" had gone and Humphrey had a beautiful pointy spike.

"From now on, my name is Spike," said Humphrey proudly. And off he went, without his box, to meet his new friends.

And do you know what? They weren't wearing boxes any more, either!

Ella's Playhouse

One hot summer's day, Ella found her dad snoozing in his deckchair.

"Dad," she called out. "I'd really like a playhouse in the garden. Will you build me one?" Ella's dad woke up and said sleepily, "Of course, Ella, anything you like."

"Will it be ready by this afternoon?" asked Ella, shaking him by the arm.

"Well, Ella, making a playhouse is not as easy as all that!" he explained. "First we'll have to draw a picture of what we want it to look like, and then..."

"That's OK, Dad. I know exactly how I want it!" said Ella. "I'll go and get my crayons."

After a while, they had finished the drawing of the playhouse. It had pink walls, four little windows and a bright red front door.

It also had curtains and a white fence around the outside.

"That's exactly right!" beamed Ella. "Now, when will it be ready?"

"Well, Ella, it's not as easy as all that," he explained. "I'll have to find some wood to make the walls and roof, and..."

"That's OK, Dad. There are lots of bits of wood in the shed. I'll help you get them."

Ella dragged him by the hand to the shed at the bottom of the garden.

After an hour, they had collected enough wood. Ella's dad was now very hot, dirty, dusty and covered in cobwebs! He was also exhausted and sat down on the sofa for a break.

"Dad, does this mean you've finished my playhouse?" Ella asked, popping her head around the door a little while later.

"Ah, well now, um… I just came in to find some of my tools…" said Dad.

"I know exactly where your tool box is," said Ella. "Come with me and I'll show you."

Dad reluctantly followed her into the garage. There, on his work bench, was a big box of tools.

"Thank you, Ella," said Dad. "Now I'll be able to start building your playhouse."

Rolling up his sleeves, he took out some tools and started building. For the rest of the afternoon, he hammered and sawed, screwed and painted, until, just as it was getting dark, he had finished the playhouse. It looked just like Ella's drawing!

"Ella will be so pleased!" Dad said to himself.

Wearily, he collected up his tools and carried the heavy box back to the house.

"I wonder where Ella is?" thought Dad.

He went into the living room, and there was Ella, fast asleep on the sofa.

"Ella," he called gently. "Wake up, Ella, your playhouse is finished!"

Ella slowly opened her eyes and yawned loudly.

"Dad," she said, "I've just had a lovely dream about a huge swimming pool in the garden! Please can you build me one of those now?"

The Selfish Puppy

Everyone adored Bonnie. She was the biggest, prettiest, cleverest puppy in the litter. Wherever she went everyone fussed over her.

However, Bonnie was also very selfish.

"Out the way," she would bark at mealtimes, as she pushed past the smaller puppies.

When it came to bedtime, she always made sure that she got the comfiest spot beside the fire.

And, worst of all, she would never let the other puppies play with the toys. Her behaviour made the other puppies cross.

One day, after Bonnie had eaten all the food without offering them so much as a nibble, they were crosser than ever.

They decided to ignore Bonnie to teach her a lesson.

After a while, Bonnie started to feel lonely, so she went to find her brothers. They were playing with a ball.

"Play with me," she said. But the other puppies ran off.

Later, she found them cuddling up next to their mother and father.

"Mum, Dad," whined Bonnie. "They won't play with me. It's not fair. After all, I am a SPECIAL puppy."

"Oh, dear," said her mother. "I think it's about time we had a little chat. You are very special," she began, "but so are Bill, Ben and Titch," said her mother.

Bonnie looked shocked.

"But they won't play with me," she whined.

"Well," said her mother. "Have you been playing nicely with them? Have you been sharing things?"

"Well...no," whispered Bonnie.

Her mother shook her head sadly. "Perhaps you should try sharing things, then you might find that your brothers will want to play with you."

"Really," whispered Bonnie, looking doubtfully at the other puppies.

Bill, Ben and Titch wagged their tails.

"And you never know," added her father. "You might even discover that sharing things is fun!"

Bonnie wasn't at all sure about this sharing thing.

But the next morning, she made sure that each puppy had an equal share of food. And in the afternoon she showed them her secret store of bones.

Bill, Ben and Titch were delighted.

Later that night, all four of them curled up together in front of the fire.

"You were right," smiled Bonnie, turning to her parents. "Sharing really is fun."

Smile, Please!

One morning, the family decided to have a family photo taken as a birthday present for Granny.

That weekend, they all put on their best clothes. It wasn't long before Mr Toogood, the photographer, arrived and set up lots of special lights in the sitting room. He asked everyone to take their places.

Everyone smiled for the camera…except Josie.

"Smile, please, Josie," Mr Toogood said.

"But this isn't all the family," said Josie and ran off to fetch Snuffles, her hamster.

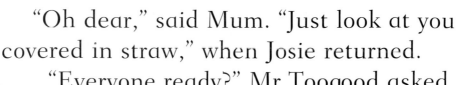

"Oh dear," said Mum. "Just look at you covered in straw," when Josie returned.

"Everyone ready?" Mr Toogood asked as they posed again. They all nodded... except Josie.

"I want Wilbur in the photo," she said. Wilbur was the family cat.

"Miaow!" wailed Wilbur, as Josie carried him back to the sofa.

"Everyone ready?" asked Mr Toogood. "Smile, please!"

"Just a minute," said Josie. "It won't be right without Cuddles." Cuddles was Josie's favourite teddy bear.

"Make it quick!" said Mum.

Josie finally found Cuddles under her bed.

"Right. Here we go, at last," said Mum, trying to stay calm.

Josie took her place on the sofa, hugging Cuddles. Wilbur purred on Mum's lap. Snuffles slept in Danny's arms. Everyone began to smile...except Josie. A big tear began to trickle down her cheek.

"Oh dear," said Mr Toogood.

"What's the matter?" asked Dad.

"Granny will be sad if Jumble isn't in the photo. She loves Jumble."

It was true. Granny did love their dog, Jumble. But no one remembered seeing him all morning. Everyone shouted his name. Then they waited.

There was a pattering sound in the hall and Jumble dashed into the sitting room. His paws were covered in dirt and his fur was very messy. He had a bone in his mouth. He leapt up onto Danny. All the other animals jumped up too!

"Woof!" Jumbles barked, as he landed on Dad's lap. He wagged his tail in Dad's face.

"Smile, PLEASE!" shouted Mr Toogood.

And Josie smiled. Everyone else burst out laughing. Mr Toogood pressed the button on his camera.

"At last!" he said.

"What will Granny think?" asked Mum.

"Granny will love it," said Josie.

And Josie was right. Granny did love the photo. It made her smile too.

The Very Serious Lion Cub

Bantu was a very serious little lion cub. He never smiled and he never ever laughed. You see, Bantu was the son of Addo, King of the Jungle, and he knew that one day he, too, would become king. And the thought of following in his father's HUGE footsteps worried Bantu.

King Addo tried his best to bring a smile to his son's face, but nothing worked.

Then, one day, King Addo decided that enough was enough. He called a jungle meeting.

"Tomorrow we're going to have a contest," he announced. "A contest to make my son, Bantu, laugh. Whoever makes him laugh first, will be made king for a day."

The jungle animals gasped. Then they started to chatter excitedly among themselves.

The following afternoon, everyone met beside the watering hole. A miserable looking Bantu sat beside his father as the other animals tried to get his attention.

The hefty hippos stumbled and bumbled their way through a hilarious ballet. Everyone watched Bantu, but his lips didn't so much as twitch.

Next to take the stage were the amazing miming chimpanzees, whose speciality was doing imitations of other jungle animals.

After the chimpanzees came the laughing hyenas, followed by the wrestling rhinos and the gyrating giraffes.

But none of the acts brought so much as a smile to Bantu's lips.

As the last giraffe waltzed off the stage, King Addo rose sadly.

"I would like to thank you all," he sighed, as he paced up and down. "But it would appear that nothing can make my little Bantu laugh."

King Addo hadn't noticed the banana skin that had been dropped in his way.

"Watch out," cried Bantu, as King Addo slipped off the bank. But he was too late.

"Ahhhhhh," roared King Addo, as he skidded on the banana skin and landed in the watering hole.

"Oooooh," gasped Bantu. Then his lips began to twitch, and his chin began to wobble. Then, much to King Addo's amazement, Bantu began to laugh.

The laughing got louder and louder, until, before long, he was rolling about on the ground.

"S…s…sorry, Father," he hiccuped. "But you just look sooooo funny. Perhaps following in your footsteps won't be so difficult, after all."